Melannie's
Book ♡

Disney BOOKS BY MAIL

© 1992 The Walt Disney Company

No portion of this book may be reproduced
without the written consent of The Walt Disney Company.

Produced by Kroha Associates, Inc.
Middletown, Connecticut

Written by M.C. Varley

Printed in the United States of America.

ISBN 1-56326-160-X

Paradise Island

One gray morning, the Little Mermaid and her friends sat in the lagoon watching the quiet, calm sea and grumbling because they had nothing to do.

"I wish I could think of something exciting to do today," sighed Ariel.

"How about a treasure hunt?" said her friend Flounder. "We could go exploring in the sunken ship!"

"We did that yesterday," Ariel replied.

"What about a picnic?" suggested Flounder's twin sister, Sandy.

Ariel sighed again. "We had one of those last week."

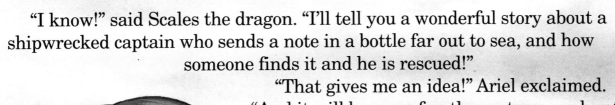

"I know!" said Scales the dragon. "I'll tell you a wonderful story about a shipwrecked captain who sends a note in a bottle far out to sea, and how someone finds it and he is rescued!"

"That gives me an idea!" Ariel exclaimed. "And it will be more fun than a treasure hunt or a picnic or even a story! I'm going to write my own letter and send it out to sea in a bottle. Maybe someone will find it and write back to *me*!"

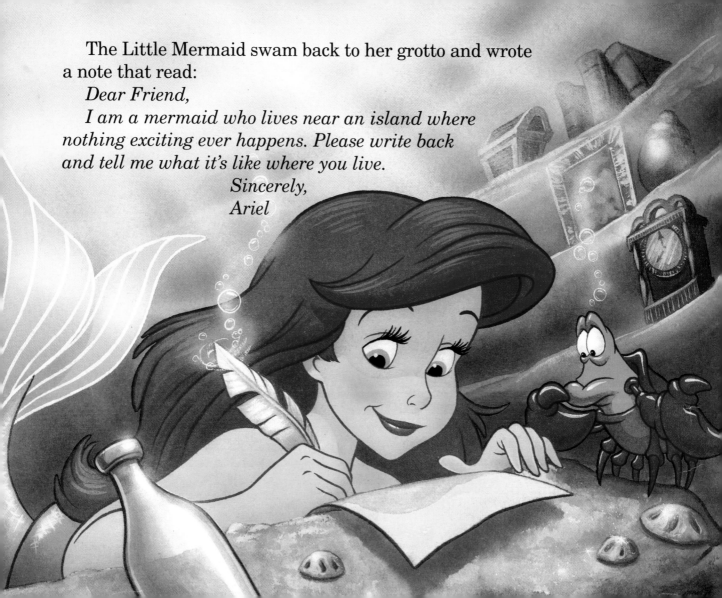

The Little Mermaid swam back to her grotto and wrote a note that read:

Dear Friend,

I am a mermaid who lives near an island where nothing exciting ever happens. Please write back and tell me what it's like where you live.

Sincerely,
Ariel

Ariel swam to the side
of the island where the
current was strong and threw the
bottle with the note as far as she could.
"I wouldn't get my hopes up," cautioned Sebastian the crab. "It's a mighty
big ocean out there. Chances are nobody will find your message."
"Oh, Sebastian," Ariel replied, "of course I'll get an answer — you'll see!"

Three days and three nights went by, and still Ariel's bottle hadn't returned.

"I told you," Sebastian said, "you're wasting your time waiting for someone to write back to you."

Just then Ariel saw the sun glinting off something in the water. "Look!" she cried.

Sebastian couldn't believe his eyes. There it was — the bottle Ariel had tossed into the sea! Could the note they saw inside be an answer to Ariel's letter?

When she got the bottle open, Ariel was thrilled to find that someone had written back to her.

Dear Ariel,

I'm sorry your island is so dull. Mine is the most unusual and interesting island in the world! There are so many fantastic things to do that my friends and I are never bored. Amazing, colorful flowers bloom all over the island. Fantastic sea shells of every shape are scattered at the edge of the clearest blue water you've ever seen. I hope you can come visit me!

Your friend,

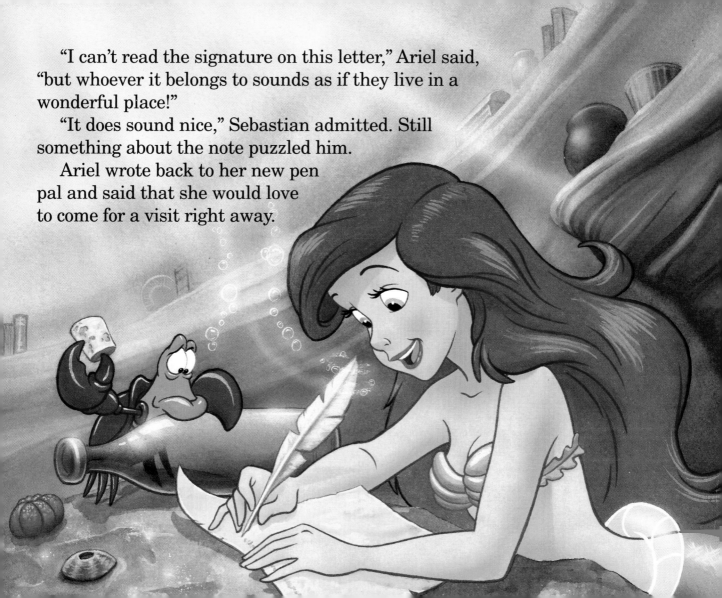

"I can't read the signature on this letter," Ariel said, "but whoever it belongs to sounds as if they live in a wonderful place!"

"It does sound nice," Sebastian admitted. Still something about the note puzzled him.

Ariel wrote back to her new pen pal and said that she would love to come for a visit right away.

A few days later, Ariel's bottle returned with a second note that read:
I'm so glad you want to see my island! I hope you'll love it as much as I do. I have lots of friends who like me very much, and I know they'll like you, too!

At the bottom of the letter was a map with instructions showing how to find the new island.

"I'm going there right now!" Ariel said as she showed the note to her friends.

"I don't know," said Sebastian. "Something just doesn't seem right to me."

"You're just upset because you said no one would write back to me and you were wrong," Ariel told him as she disappeared with a splash.

Just then Sebastian saw
something moving behind the
rocks. It was Ursula the evil sea witch! *I wonder what she's doing
here?* Sebastian thought, as he watched her slink slowly to the depths
of the sea. *I better follow her and find out.*

When Sebastian reached
Ursula's cave, he saw the
notes Ariel had sent in her bottle!
"My plan worked!" Sebastian overheard
Ursula cackle to her eels, Flotsam and Jetsam. "The
Little Mermaid is gone forever! She can never find that island,
because I made it all up! And best of all, my map will lead her straight to
a deep, black whirlpool. She'll be pulled down into it and trapped forever."

So it was a trick! I knew something about those letters was strange, Sebastian thought as he raced back to the lagoon to tell the others.

"Scuttle, it is up to you to find Ariel and warn her! According to the map, she must have gone that way!" Sebastian said, pointing out to sea.

"Don't worry. I'll save her!" cried Scuttle as he took off.

"And hurry!" Sebastian called out. "Hurry!"

Scuttle flew harder and faster than he had ever flown before, searching the ocean for any sign of Ariel. *What if I'm too late?* he thought, swooping in low for a closer look.

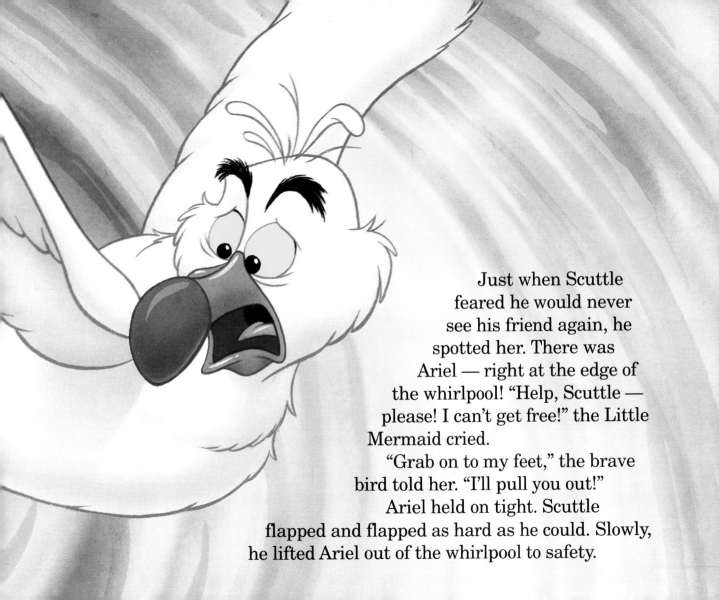

Just when Scuttle
feared he would never
see his friend again, he
spotted her. There was
Ariel — right at the edge of
the whirlpool! "Help, Scuttle —
please! I can't get free!" the Little
Mermaid cried.

"Grab on to my feet," the brave
bird told her. "I'll pull you out!"

Ariel held on tight. Scuttle
flapped and flapped as hard as he could. Slowly,
he lifted Ariel out of the whirlpool to safety.

When Scuttle and Ariel were safely back in the lagoon, Sebastian explained to the Little Mermaid what Ursula had done.

"What a horrible trick!" Ariel exclaimed.

"I can't believe even Ursula would do such a thing!" said Sandy.

"If it weren't for Scuttle and Sebastian, I don't know how I would have escaped. I'm so glad to be back here with all of you," the Little Mermaid said gratefully.

"I certainly hope you will think twice before running off to someplace you think is better than here," Sebastian added.

"That note Ursula wrote about the fantastic island reminds me of *our* island," said Scales.

"Our flowers are beautiful," added Scuttle as he placed a necklace of them around Ariel's neck.

"And our sea shells are beautiful, too!" Sandy said.

"You're right!" Ariel said with a smile. "Imagine that — it was Ursula's trick that made me realize what a special place my own island is, and what special friends you all are! Scuttle, find that bottle — I want to send Ursula a thank you note!"